THE TERRIBLE
UNDERPANTS

YIKES!

Real hairy-nosed wombats don't live with little girls, they live in the bush. If you would like to help wombats such as the threatened Northern Hairy-nosed Wombat, you can help try to protect the places where wombats need to live. You can contact:

World Wide Fund for Nature Australia
Threatened Species Network,
GPO Box 528, Sydney, NSW 2001.

The Australian Conservation Foundation
Land Clearing Campaign,
340 Gore Street, Fitzroy, Victoria 3065.

THE TERRIBLE UNDERPANTS

Written and Illustrated by
Kaz Cooke

HYPERION BOOKS FOR CHILDREN
NEW YORK

My name is Wanda-Linda,
and this is Glenda.
She is a hairy-nosed wombat.

"Wanda-Linda and Glenda!"
my dad called out one morning.
"It's time to get dressed."

(Actually, because Glenda is
a hairy-nosed wombat,
she hardly ever gets dressed.)

I put on a dress,
but I couldn't find any underpants.

"Mom," I said, "where are all my underpants?"

"Ask your dad," Mom said.

"Dad," I said, "where are all my underpants?"

"Ask your mom," Dad said.

"Um. Are they in the washing machine?"
Mom asked.

"NO!" I said.

"Did I hang them on the line?"
Dad called out.

"YES!" I yelled back.

"You can't wear wet undies," Mom said.
"How about these?"

OH, NO!
NOT THE TERRIBLE UNDERPANTS!

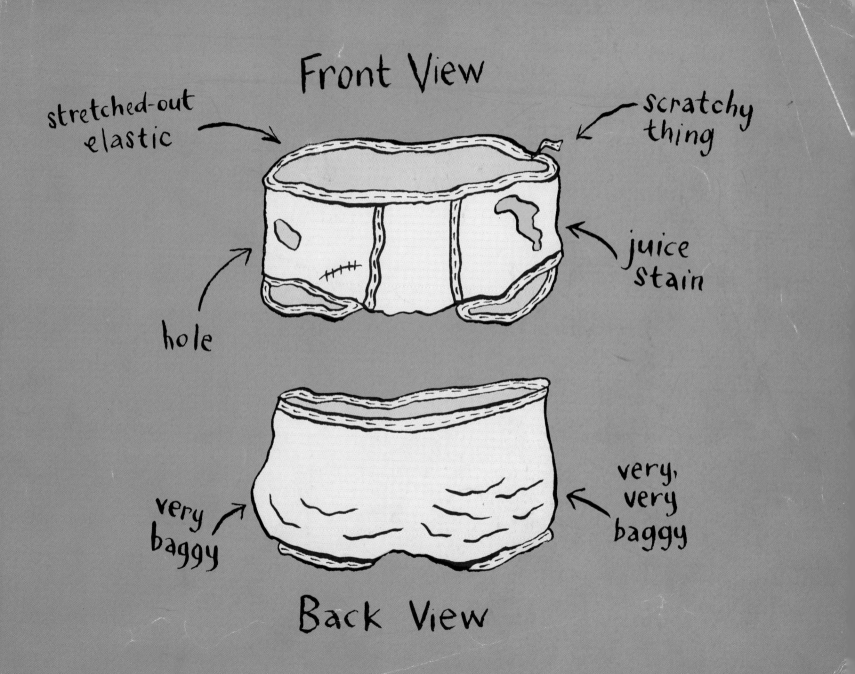

I wish I had a pair of
Perfectly Wonderful Underpants instead.

"Never mind," said Dad.
"Nobody will notice the Terrible Underpants."

"Quite frankly," I replied,
"I find that very difficult to believe."

We went to the shop, and a big gust of wind
blew up my dress.
Mrs. Kafoops from down the street saw
the Terrible Underpants.

"My stars, Wanda-Linda," she said.
"What a frightful pair of underpants."

When I got home I ran through
the sprinkler to cool down,
and Mom said, "Those really are
Terrible Underpants, Wanda-Linda."

"I KNOW!" I said.

———

I did a handstand,
and somebody in a helicopter took a picture
and put it on the TV.
And EVERYBODY in the WHOLE WORLD saw
the Terrible Underpants.

So I took them off.

THE END